"Remember the rules," said Sheriff Lewis.
"The pups find the eggs. The kids pick them up."

"Go!" said Sheriff Lewis.
Charley went with T-Bone.
Vaz went with Cleo.

Clifford™
THE BIG EGG HUNT

Latisha

Written by Suzanne Weyn
Illustrated by Jim Durk

SCHOLASTIC

It was the day of the big Kids and Pups
Egg Hunt.

Jetta went with Mac.
And Emily Elizabeth went with Clifford.
The dogs sniffed and sniffed.

Clifford was the first to find some eggs.
They were high up in a tree.
"Woof!" he barked.

Emily Elizabeth giggled.
"We can't take these eggs," she said.
"They belong to Mrs Robin!"

T-Bone saw an egg under a bench.

But before he had a chance to bark,
Cleo barked and Vaz picked up the egg.

Then T-Bone saw an egg on the slide.

But before he had a chance to bark,
Clifford barked and Emily Elizabeth picked
up the egg.

T-Bone saw an egg behind a rock.

But before he had a chance to bark,
Mac barked and Jetta picked up the egg.

After a while, everyone had lots of eggs –
everyone except T-Bone and Charley.
They didn't have any.

"I'm so unlucky," T-Bone said to Clifford.
"You can have some of my eggs," said Clifford.
"No thanks," said T-Bone. "I want to find the
eggs myself."

Then Clifford had an idea.
"Let's hide some of our eggs where T-Bone
can find them," he said.
Mac didn't think this was fair.

"But it would make T-Bone happy," said Cleo.

"Oh, all right," said Mac.

"How will we get the kids to help?" Cleo asked.

"Just watch me," said Clifford.

Clifford walked over to Emily Elizabeth.
He carefully tipped over her basket and
one of the eggs fell out.

Clifford rolled the egg into the tall grass.

T-Bone found it right away!
"Woof!" he barked and Charley picked it up.

Cleo walked over to Vaz.
She carefully tipped over his basket and
one of the eggs fell out.

Cleo rolled it over to a tree.

T-Bone found that one, too!
"Woof!" he barked and Charley picked it up.

Then Mac tipped over Jetta's basket.

He rolled one of her eggs into some leaves.

"Woof!" T-Bone barked and Charley picked
up the egg.

Soon T-Bone and Charley had as many eggs as their friends.

"You have lots of eggs now," Clifford said
to T-Bone. "You *are* lucky, after all!"
"I am lucky," said T-Bone, "but not because
I found these eggs. I know what you did.

You put the eggs where I could find them. I'm lucky because I have good friends who want me to be happy. Thanks, guys!"

So everyone ate the eggs.
And everyone was happy!

Other Clifford Storybooks:

The Big Leaf Pile
The Runaway Rabbit
The Show-and-Tell Surprise
Tummy Trouble

Scholastic Children's Books
Commonwealth House, 1-19 New Oxford Street, London WC1A 1NU
a division of Scholastic Ltd
London ~ New York ~ Toronto ~ Sydney ~ Auckland ~ Mexico City ~ New Delhi ~ Hong Kong

First published in the USA by Scholastic Inc., 2002
This edition published in the UK by Scholastic Ltd, 2003

ISBN 0 439 97869 6

Based on the CLIFFORD THE BIG RED DOG book series published by Scholastic Inc.™ & © Norman Bridwell.
CLIFFORD and associated logos are trademarks and/or registered trademarks of Norman Bridwell.

1 2 3 4 5 6 7 8 9 10 Printed in Italy by Amadeus S.p.A. - Rome